# Ricky, Karim and Spit Nolan

ADVENTURE SHORT STORIES

## Contents

Series editors: Martin Coles and Christine Hall

PEARSON EDUCATION LIMITED
Edinburgh Gate
Harlow
Essex CM20 2JE
England

www.longman.co.uk



We are grateful to Nelson Thornes Ltd for permission to reproduce the story 'Spit Nolan' by Bill Naughton from *The Goalkeeper's Revenge and Other Stories* by Bill Naughton



First published 2003
ISBN 0582 79613 X

Illustrated by Linda Clark (The Black & White Line), Nilesh Mistry and Susan Hellard (Arena)

Printed in Great Britain by Scotprint, Haddington

The publishers' policy is to use paper manufactured from sustainable forests.

# Spit Nolan

by Bill Naughton

Spit Nolan was a pal of mine. He was a thin lad with a bony face that was always pale, except for two rosy spots on his cheekbones. He had quick brown eyes, short, wiry hair, rather stooped shoulders, and we all knew that he had only one lung. He had had a disease which in those days couldn't be cured, unless you went away to Switzerland, which Spit certainly couldn't afford. He wasn't sorry for himself in any way, and in fact we envied him, because he never had to go to school.

Spit was the champion trolley-rider of Cotton Pocket; that was the district in which we lived. He had very good balance, and sharp wits, and he was very brave, so that these qualities, when added to his skill as a rider, meant that no other boy could ever beat Spit on a trolley – and every lad had one.

Our trolleys were simple vehicles for getting a

good ride downhill at a fast speed. To make one you had to get a stout piece of wood about five feet in length and eighteen inches wide. Then you needed four wheels, preferably two pairs – large ones for the back and smaller ones for the front. However, since we bought our wheels from the scrapyard, most trolleys had four odd wheels. Now you had to get a poker and put it in the fire until it was red hot, and then burn a hole through the wood at the front.

Usually it would take three or four attempts to get the hole bored through. Through this hole you fitted the giant nut and bolt, which acted as a swivel for the steering. Fastened to the nut was a strip of wood, onto which the front axle was secured by bent nails. A piece of rope tied to each end of the axle served for steering. Then, a knob of margarine had to be slanced out of the kitchen to grease the wheels and bearings. Next you had to paint a name on it: *Invincible* or *Dreadnought*, though it might be a motto: *Death Before Dishonour* or *Labour and Wait*. That done, you then stuck your chest out, opened the back gate and wheeled your trolley out to face the critical eyes of the world.

Spit spent most mornings trying out new speed gadgets on his trolley, or searching Enty's scrapyard for good wheels. Afterwards he would go off and have a spin down Cemetery Brew. This was a very steep road that led to the cemetery, and it was very popular with trolley-drivers as it was the only macadamized hill for miles around, all the others being cobblestones for horse traffic. Spit used to lie in wait for a coal cart or other horse-drawn vehicle, then he would hitch *Egdam* to the back to take it up the brew. *Egdam* was a name in memory of a girl called Madge, whom he had once met at Southport Sanatorium, where he had spent three happy weeks. Only I knew the meaning of it, for he had reversed the letters of her name to keep his love a secret.

It was the custom for lads to gather at the street corner on summer evenings and, trolleys parked at hand, discuss trolleying, road surfaces, and also show off any new gadgets. Then, when Spit gave

Brew: hill
macadamized: covered in tarmac
Sanatorium: a kind of hospital for sick people who need to rest while getting better

the sign, we used to set off for Cemetery Brew. There was scarcely any evening traffic on the roads in those days, so that we could have a good practice before our evening race. Spit, the unbeaten champion, would inspect every trolley and rider, and allow a start which was reckoned on the size of the wheels and the weight of the rider. He was always the last in the line of starters, though no matter how long a start he gave it seemed impossible to beat him. He knew that road like the palm of his hand, every tiny lump or pothole, and he never came a cropper.

Among us he took things easy, but when occasion asked for it he would go all out. Once he had to meet a challenge from Ducker Smith, the champion of the Engine Row gang. On that occasion Spit borrowed a wheel from the baby's pram, removing one nearest the wall, so it wouldn't be missed, and confident he could replace it before his mother took baby out. And after fixing it to his trolley he made that ride on what was called the 'belly-down' style – that is, he lay full stretch on his stomach, so as to avoid wind resistance. Although Ducker got away with a flying start he had not that sensitive touch of Spit, and his frequent bumps and swerves lost him valuable inches, so that he lost the race with a good three lengths. Spit arrived home just in time to catch his mother as she was wheeling young Georgie off the doorstep, and if he had not made a dash for it the child would have fallen out as the pram overturned.

* * * * *

It happened that we were gathered at the street corner with our trolleys one evening when Ernie Haddock let out a hiccup of wonder: "Hey, chaps, wot's Leslie got?"

We all turned our eyes on Leslie Duckett, the plump son of the local publican. He approached us on a brand-new trolley, propelled by flicks of his foot on the pavement. From a distance the thing had looked impressive, but now, when it came up among us, we were too dumbfounded to speak.

Such a magnificent trolley had never been seen! The riding board was of solid oak, almost two inches thick; four new wheels with pneumatic tyres; a brake, a bell, a lamp, and a spotless steering-cord. In front was a plate on which was the name in bold lettering: *The British Queen*.

"It's called after the pub," remarked Leslie. He tried to edge it away from Spit's trolley, for it made *Egdam* appear horribly insignificant. Voices had been stilled for a minute, but now they broke out:

"Where'd it come from?"

"How much was it?"

"Who made it?"

Leslie tried to look modest. "My dad had it specially made to measure," he said, "by the gaffer of the Holt Engineering Works."

gaffer: boss

He was a nice lad, and now he wasn't sure whether to feel proud or ashamed. The fact was, nobody had ever had a trolley made by somebody else. Trolleys were swapped and so on, but no lad had ever owned one that had been made by other hands. We went quiet now, for Spit had calmly turned his attention to it, and was examining *The British Queen* with his expert eye. First he tilted it, so that one of the rear wheels was off the ground, and after giving it a flick of the finger he listened intently with his ear close to the hub.

"A beautiful ball bearing race," he remarked. "It runs like silk." Next he turned his attention to the body. "Grand piece of timber, Leslie – though a trifle on the heavy side.

It'll take plenty of pulling up a brew."

"I can pull it," said Leslie, stiffening.

"You might find it a shade *front-heavy*," went on Spit, "which means it'll be hard on the steering unless you keep it well oiled."

"It's well made," said Leslie. "Eh, Spit?"

Spit nodded. "Aye, all the bolts are countersunk," he said, "everything chamfered and fluted off to perfection. But –"

"But what?" asked Leslie.

"Do you want me to tell you?" asked Spit.

"Yes, I do," answered Leslie.

"Well, it's got none of *you* in it," said Spit.

"How do you mean?" says Leslie.

"Well, you haven't so much as given it a single tap with a hammer," said Spit. "That trolley will be a stranger to you to your dying day."

"How come," said Leslie, "since I *own* it?"

Spit shook his head. "You don't own it," he said, in a quiet, solemn tone. "You own nothing in

chamfered: with corners made of wood
fluted: decorated with parallel grooves

this world except those things you have taken a hand in the making of, or else you've earned the money to buy them."

Leslie sat down on *The British Queen* to think this one out. We all sat round, scratching our heads.

"You've forgotten to mention one thing," said Ernie Haddock to Spit, "what about the *speed?*"

"Going down a steep hill," said Spit, "she should hold the road well – an' with wheels like that she should certainly be able to shift some."

"Think she could beat *Egdam*?" ventured Ernie.

"That," said Spit, "remains to be seen."

Ernie gave a shout. "A challenge race! *The British Queen* versus *Egdam*!"

"Not tonight," said Leslie. "I haven't got the proper feel of her yet."

"What about Sunday morning?" I said.

Spit nodded. "As good a time as any."

Leslie agreed. "By then," he said in a challenging tone, "I'll be able to handle her."

* * * * *

Chattering like monkeys, eating bread, carrots, fruit, and bits of toffee, the entire gang of us made our way along the silent Sunday-morning streets for the big race at Cemetery Brew. We were split into two fairly equal sides.

Leslie, in his serge Sunday suit,

walked ahead, with Ernie Haddock pulling *The British Queen*, and a bunch of supporters around. They were optimistic, for Leslie had easily outpaced every other trolley during the week, though as yet he had not run against Spit.

Spit was in the middle of the group behind, and I was pulling *Egdam* and keeping the pace easy, for I wanted Spit to keep fresh. He walked in and out among us with an air of imperturbability that, considering the occasion, seemed almost godlike.

It inspired a fanatical confidence in us. It was such that Chick Dale, a curly-headed kid with a soft skin like a girl's, and a nervous lisp, climbed up on to the spiked railings of the cemetery, and, reaching out with his thin fingers, snatched a yellow rose. He ran in front of Spit and thrust it into a small hole in his jersey.

"I pwesent you, with the wose of the winner!" he exclaimed.

"And I've a good mind to present you with a clout on the lug," replied Spit, "for pinching a flower from a cemetery. An' what's more, it's bad luck." Seeing Chick's face, he relented. "On second thoughts, Chick, I'll wear it. Ee, wot a 'eavenly smell!"

Happily we went along, and Spit turned to a couple of lads at the back. "Hey, stop that whistling. Don't forget what day it is – folk want their sleep out."

A faint sweated glow had come over Spit's face when we reached the top of the hill, but he was as majestically calm as ever. Taking the bottle of cold water from his trolley seat, he put it to his lips and rinsed out his mouth in the manner of a boxer.

clout: a hard slap
lug: ear

The two contestants were called together by Ernie. “No bumpin’ or borin’,” he said.

They nodded.

“The winner,” he said, “is the first who puts the nose of his trolley past the cemetery gates.”

They nodded.

“Now, who,” he asked, “is to be judge?”

Leslie looked at me. “I’ve no objection to Bill,” he said. “I know he’s straight.”

I hadn’t realised I was, I thought, ‘but by heck I will be!’

“Ernie here,” said Spit, “can be starter.”

With that Leslie and Spit shook hands.

“Fly down to them gates,” said Ernie to me. He had his father’s pigeon-timing watch in his hand. “I’ll be setting ’em off dead on the stroke of ten o’clock.”

I hurried down to the gates. I looked back and saw the supporters lining themselves on either side of the road. Leslie was sitting upright on *The British Queen*. Spit was settling himself to ride belly down. Ernie Haddock, handkerchief raised in the right hand, eyes gazing down on the watch

in the left, was counting them off – just like when he tossed one of his father's pigeons.

"Five – four – three – two – one – *off*!"

Spit was away like a shot. That vigorous toe push sent him clean ahead of Leslie. A volley of shouts went up from his supporters, and groans from Leslie's. I saw Spit move straight to the middle of the road camber. Then I ran ahead to take up my position at the winning post.

When I turned again I was surprised to see that Spit had not increased the lead. In fact, it seemed that Leslie had begun to gain on him. He had settled himself into a crouched position, and those perfect wheels combined with his extra weight were bringing him up with Spit. Not that it seemed possible he could ever catch him. For Spit, lying flat on his trolley, moving with a fine balance, gliding, as it were, over the rough patches, looked to me as though he were a bird that might suddenly open out its wings and fly clean into the air.

The runners along the side could no longer keep up with the trolleys. And now, as they

camber: a slight upward curve towards the centre of a road

skimmed past the halfway mark, and came to the very steepest part, there was no doubt that Leslie was gaining. Spit had never ridden better; he coaxed *Egdam* over the tricky parts, swayed with her, gave her her head, and guided her. Yet Leslie, clinging grimly to the steering rope of *The British Queen*, and riding the rougher part of the road, was actually drawing level. Those beautiful ball bearing wheels, engineer-made, encased in oil, were holding the road, and bringing Leslie along faster than spirit and skill could carry Spit.

Dead level they sped into the final stretch. Spit's slight figure was poised fearlessly on his trolley, drawing the extremes of speed from her. Thundering beside him, anxious but determined, came Leslie. He was actually drawing ahead – and forcing his way to the top of the camber. On they came like two charioteers – Spit delicately edging to the side, to gain inches by the extra downward momentum. I kept my eyes fastened clean across the road as they came belting past the winning post.

First past was the plate of *The British Queen*. I saw that first. Then I saw the heavy rear wheel jog over a pothole and strike Spit's front wheel – sending him in a swerve across the road. Suddenly then, from nowhere, a charabanc came speeding round the wide bend.

Spit was straight in its path. Nothing could avoid the collision. I gave a cry of fear as I saw the heavy solid tyre of the front wheel hit the trolley. Spit was flung up and his back hit the radiator. Then the driver stopped dead.

I got there first. Spit was lying on the macadam road on his side. His face was white and dusty, and coming out between his lips, and trickling down his chin, was a rivulet of fresh red blood. Scattered all about him were yellow rose petals.

charabanc: an old-fashioned large bus used for day trips

"Not my fault," I heard the driver shouting. "I didn't have a chance. He came straight at me."

The next thing we were surrounded by women who had got out of the charabanc. And then Leslie and all the lads came up.

"Somebody send for an ambulance!" called a woman.

"I'll run an' tell the gatekeeper to telephone," said Ernie Haddock.

"I hadn't a chance," the driver explained to the women.

"A piece of his jersey on the starting-handle there ..." said someone.

"Don't move him," said the driver to a stout woman who had bent over Spit. "Wait for the ambulance."

"Hush up," she said. She knelt and put a silk scarf under Spit's head. Then she wiped his mouth with her little handkerchief.

He opened his eyes. Glazed they were, as though he couldn't see. A short cough came out of him, then he looked at me and his lips moved.

"Who won?"

"Thee!" blurted out Leslie. "Tha just licked me. Eh, Bill?"

"Aye," I said, "old *Egdam* just pipped *The British Queen*."

starting-handle: a handle found at the front of old cars and buses that was turned to make the motor start

Spit's eyes closed again. The women looked at each other. They nearly all had tears in their eyes. Then Spit looked up again, and his wise, knowing look came over his face. After a minute he spoke in a sharp whisper:

"Liars. I can remember seeing Leslie's back wheel hit my front 'un. I didn't win – I lost." He stared upward for a few seconds, then his eyes twitched and shut.

The driver kept repeating how it wasn't his fault, and next thing the ambulance came. Nearly all the women were crying now, and I saw the look that went between the two men who put Spit on a stretcher – but I couldn't believe he was dead. I had to go into the ambulance with the attendant to give him particulars. I went up the step and sat down inside and looked out the little window as the driver slammed the doors.

I saw the driver holding Leslie as a witness. Chick Dale was lifting the smashed-up *Egdam* onto the body of *The British Queen*. People with bunches of flowers in their hands stared after us as we drove off. Then I heard the ambulance man asking me Spit's name. Then he touched me on the elbow with his pencil and said, "Where did he live?"

I knew then. That word 'did' struck right into me. But for a minute I couldn't answer. I had to think hard, for the way he said it made it suddenly seem as though Spit Nolan had been dead and gone for ages.

# Thunderball Badshah

by Pratima Mitchell

Karim could feel his skin burning with excitement. Unfortunately, it wasn't the kind of tingling thrill he got when he went to the circus or a fair. It wasn't the feeling that burst into his lungs when he scored a goal, or even when he freewheeled dangerously down the twisty Amber Hill road. This was a feverish hectic excitement, fuelled by a warning: 'just two hours before the sun goes down; only two hours to finish gluing his kite *Thunderball*, to try a test flight, correct any problems and be calm and ready for the big day tomorrow.' Taking a deep breath, Karim's fingers fairly flew to complete the many remaining tasks, which involved complicated knots and fussing with a thick flour and water paste.

Early next morning was Jaipur city's annual kite-flying competition, and Karim had a lot invested in winning the junior section for the first time. If he won, his Uncle Hamid had promised to take him on a trip to Delhi on the train. He said he would go with him to the Indira Gandhi International Airport, where he could watch planes take off and land for a whole afternoon. Karim's father had said he would contribute as many rupees as the prize money so he could have a new bike.

Besides, he had to beat that smug toad Keshav next door. Not only was he top in maths and science, he was always bragging about his older brother who was studying in the USA. All in all, there was a lot at stake.

He checked his watch. The minutes were ticking by. Once the sun went down behind Amber Hill Fort he'd have to pack up and go home to his family's tiny apartment with babies and beds and cooking and brothers and sisters running in and out, and Amma shouting and sending him on last minute errands to the grocer downstairs. There'd be nowhere to work on *Thunderball.*

So he had to make good use of this time in Mira's courtyard, which lay directly under the ancient city wall.

On the ground was the kite frame – sticks of finest bamboo tied together with white sewing cotton. The kite was ready to assemble, but he had to work slowly, carefully, with a steady, delicate touch. His fingers were just poised to cut a length of gossamer-thin scarlet silk, when something flew past his ear and landed on the template. The paper moved slightly and the scissors dropped from his hand, nicking the cloth.

Karim swore in his head. Mira was pelting him with potato peelings. Perched high above on the old wall, she teased, "Let me, let me ..." She had the advantage from her eyrie. The wall had been built in medieval times to guard the city against invaders. It ran all along one side of Mira's house. From its thirty-feet height she had a fantastic view of the old city, with its higgledy-piggledy back lanes full of noise and adventure and excitement.

"Let me, let me ..." she sang, so that Karim had to

grit his teeth to stop himself shouting at her.

"Let you what?" he said, forcing patience into his tone and smoothing out the cloth again. Three parts red and one part black. Tomorrow *Thunderball Badshah* – Thunderball the Emperor – was going to strike terror in the hearts of all the other competitors.

"Let me have a go at killing kites tomorrow," Mira pleaded.

He turned his head to squint up. "If you keep on worrying me, there will be no competition for us. Look how much work there is to finish ... just leave me alone for now. Okay?"

He had to be careful not to annoy her, or else there'd be nowhere for him to work. Mira had her uses. At least she had the sense to keep her voice down and not squawk loud enough for Keshav to hear. Also, she was able to see into Keshav's courtyard, and she kept Karim up-to-date with his rival's plans. Apparently Keshav was fixing tiny balls of soft lead to his kite frame. Launching wouldn't be that easy, but once up, the lead ballast would give Keshav's kite terrific balance and steering.

But Karim wasn't blinded by the engineering. He had a trick or two up his own sleeve. He had made a deal with the sweet-maker round the corner of the lane, who squatted over his bubbling cauldrons of condensed milk and sticky sugar syrup all day. The sweet-maker had moved his three chins up and down. Translated, this meant that Karim could steam the bamboo sticks over his huge vat of boiling water. Karim had never seen the man speak. His chins either nodded up and down for 'yes', or wobbled sideways for 'no'. As Karim's bamboo kite frame softened, he'd bent the crossbar into an aerodynamic curve. Tomorrow *Thunderball* was going to swoop on the back of air currents! It was going to dive-bomb into the airborne fleet of flimsy tissue paper! Lord of the skies, it would first hover like a bird of prey, and then ... zap! Snapping at their mooring strings, *Thunderball* would bring his rivals' kites tumbling down, defeated. Last year Keshav had cut down three kites. This year Karim was determined to beat that score. He could almost hear the roar of the crowd echoing all over Jaipur, "Karim is the winner! Karim is the champion!"

He came back to earth when another potato peeling hit his ear. "Say you'll let me fly *Thunderball* tomorrow, say it!"

It was too much. Just because she let him work in her courtyard didn't give Mira the right to bully him. Anyway, girls never flew kites in the competition. They just never had done. What on earth would his friends say?

Mira's mother called from inside the kitchen, "Lazy girl! Are those potatoes peeled?"

Mira took a last look at the late afternoon bustle of the city spread below her. A glorious cacophony of sound drifted up – honking horns, tinkling rickshaw bells, bargain-proclaiming fruit-sellers, a wedding band practising wonky wrong notes. Swoops of bright green parrots flashed past her and the aroma of frying bhajis tickled her nose. Screwing her eyes against the setting sun she tried to make out if her grandfather's camel cart was somewhere to be seen. Plodding through the traffic she sighted a few pompous-looking camels, even an elephant or two, but no sign yet of Grandfather.

But every year he came for the kite-flying festival, because he'd been a champion in his youth. He came with his flat-bedded cart laden with sacks of presents from their village: yellow lentils, good wheat flour, cornmeal, hub-shaped disks of golden coloured raw sugar, sugar cane sticks for Mira, and a basket of potatoes and onions. Tomorrow, he and Mira would climb up to their rooftop and together watch the red, green, purple and yellow kites dancing like butterflies in the clear blue sky.

* * * * *

Karim held up his finished kite to catch the last rays of the sun filtering through the leaves of the guava tree. At last, all was ready for the test flight. He dodged Mira, and carrying *Thunderball* like a trophy above his head, climbed up the granite steps to the top of the wall.

Falcons glided effortlessly above. He'd studied the birds for hours to try and work out how they mastered air currents. It was the resilient strength of the wing bone, buoyed by the lightness of the feathers that provided the blueprint for his own design: young bamboo sticks, like bone, covered with the finest silk from Uncle Hamid's shop. *Thunderball* should fly like a falcon.

He flexed the bamboo crossbar ready, alert to

the first friendly breeze, then launched his kite. He allowed it some play with the twine, feeling its belly pushing against the wind. Up and up it soared now, in brilliant form. It was thrilling to watch the aerodynamic shape turning in the sky. He let it ride for a while, Mira clapping her hands joyfully at his side, and then started to reel it in again – like playing with a fish in the river. No hurry, nice and easy, gently, gently like you entice a peacock to come and peck the grain in your open palm.

But, all of a sudden, a freak wind, with a sting of desert sand in its tail, caught the kite and clipped it rudely, bringing it down towards the middle of the courtyard. It plummeted like a shot bird, getting stuck in the very top branches of the guava tree. Karim's heart also plummeted. He couldn't tell whether the kite was damaged. He couldn't reach it because it was so high up in the branches. Even if they'd had a ladder tall enough he couldn't have climbed it. His left leg didn't have enough strength because he'd had polio when he was small. Keshav could have shinned up the tree, but there was no way he was going to ask him!

Just then, the gentle clunk-clunk of camel bells sounded in the lane outside the courtyard.

"Dadaji!" Mira shouted, abandoning the disaster to run and tell her grandfather the bad news.

Dadaji climbed down from his cart. "I saw, I saw. It was flying well. But where will you find a ladder at this time of night?"

Mira's mother brought a bucket of water for the camel and Dadaji sloshed some of it on its big dusty feet. He unbridled the camel and led it to be tethered under the guava tree. A happy smile seemed to spread over the camel's face when it saw the juicy guava leaves.

"No you don't!" Mira smacked it on its rump.

She put her hands on her hips. "Karim, I can get your kite down, but I'll only risk my neck on one condition."

"Which is?"

"That I share the kite-flying with you tomorrow, and you take me with you to watch the planes at the airport in Delhi."

Karim's mouth stayed open. He could not believe her boldness. Anyway, she was just a bigmouth. How on earth would she get up the tree?

"Hup hup heee!" Mira thumped the camel again and it folded its front legs obediently and sat down. She climbed on its back. "Hup hup hooo!" and the beast clambered up again to its full height with Mira on top.

"If I stand up, I can get the kite. Come on, Karim, promise, or I'm coming down again."

Sweat formed on Karim's forehead. "It's blackmail!" he shouted angrily.

"Go on, Karim, don't be silly or you'll lose your kite. Say yes to Mira," said Mira's mum.

"You'll allow her to go to Delhi with Hamid Chacha and me?"

"Yes, why not? You're friends, aren't you?"

Desperation drove Karim to agree. "But I'll have the first turn! You can have a go after I've brought down four kites."

"We have two witnesses," Mira replied. "Don't you dare change your mind!"

She raised herself slowly up, wobbling a little on her bare feet. Dadaji held the bridle. It was a brave thing to do.

Gently she disentangled *Thunderball* and sat

down again on the saddle before examining the silk for tears. "It's fine," she pronounced, handing it back to Karim and jumping off the now seated camel. She broke off a piece of raw brown sugar from one of the golden hubs and let the camel nibble it from her hand.

* * * * *

The day of the competition dawned. It was the last day of winter. In Jaipur, everyone loves the winter months because the sun is so comforting, the air so crisp and the flowers bloom riotously.

Only those competitors whose names were on the official list were allowed to fly their kites that morning. They were all gathered on their rooftops making last-minute adjustments to their kites. Each competitor was accompanied by a badge-wearing official, to make sure the kills were fair, and to keep a tally. The judges waited for the last stroke of nine from the clocktower and a gunshot went off to signal the start of the competition.

Karim had two other kites lined up, also in his

colours of red and black, but made of conventional tissue paper. He let Mira hold *Thunderball* to launch it. Away it went, spinning higher and higher, with Karim dodging about on the roof steering it into the thermals above. He set his first target and stalked it: with a tug of his twine he guided *Thunderball* to cut into a white kite. Down it came. Dadaji and Mira whooped happily. They could see Keshav on his own rooftop with his family cheering him on. The brother from America was home on holiday wearing a baggy sweatshirt with *'BOSTON UNIVERSITY'* written across the front.

Karim followed his first hit by bringing down two others – a yellow, and a blue and purple. He launched *Thunderball* again. Mira held the spool for him; she followed his every move to allow him flexibility for whichever way he wanted to dodge about. This time Keshav turned his attention to Karim's kite, challenging him directly with an orange kite. There was no doubt about it, Keshav was a very skilful kite-flyer. *Thunderball* and Keshaw's kite were flying at the same height,

not too close, waiting for the right moment to strike. They could have been at a village fair and not competing in one of the premier kite-flying competitions in India.

Quietly, Mira's voice sounded right behind Karim. "Kill it," she urged. "Go on, *now*!"

Somehow, her timing must have been perfect, because when Karim tugged his twine to change direction swiftly, he caught Keshav unaware. It was a matter of a split second, but it made the difference. Down came the orange kite amid groans and shouts of disappointment from Keshav's relations.

"That's four –

now it's my turn," Mira said triumphantly.

Karim was hopping with impatience. Keshav and he had drawn – four kites each. "I have to get more than *him*," he protested.

"A promise is a promise," Mira shouted defiantly. She snatched the twine from him and handed him the spool to unreel.

"Only three minutes more," the official said pompously.

Once more, *Thunderball* was launched into the air. The breeze was stiffer now and it climbed up true and straight. Mira handled the kite with an expert flick of her wrist, making it dart here and there to chase Keshav's.

She moved with the grace of a dancer on the balls of her feet, and her expression was one of intense concentration.

Reluctantly, Karim had to admit that Mira's skills weren't bad. She took risks like him, and in

no time she'd brought down one more.

"Enough! End of time!" the official insisted, writing down the score.

Karim's *Thunderball* won the juniors by a margin of one. Keshav was second with four hits.

* * * * *

Karim bought his bike, a red one with ten gears and a fancy horn that played 'Yankee Doodle Dandy' and drove everyone mad.

Uncle Hamid took Mira and Karim to the Indira Gandhi International Airport, where they watched dozens and dozens of planes taking off and landing.

"I'll be on one of those when I'm older," Karim said to Mira.

"I'll be *flying* them when I'm grown up," she replied witheringly.

"Now why didn't I think of that?" Karim said to himself.

Being good at kite-flying didn't mean that she was going to become an airline pilot. He'd have to keep his eye on her to make sure she didn't get too big for her sandals!

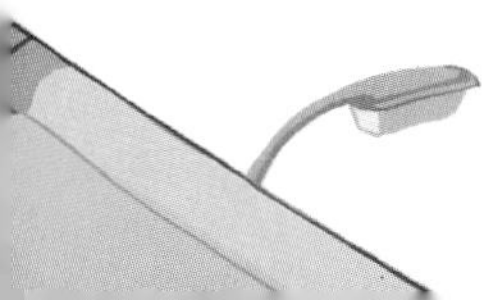

# Ricky's Wheels

by Jenny Alexander

Every day after school we race home through the park, Ricky and me, and nine times out of ten Ricky wins. When we first started doing it, it used to be ten times out of ten, but then I stopped taking pity on him on the shallow uphill slope before the bandstand, because he certainly didn't take pity on me on the long roll downhill towards the lake.

Sometimes people give me a dirty look when they see Ricky pushing up the hill, and me haring on ahead. "Shame on you!" they say. "Why aren't you helping your friend?" That makes me and Ricky really cross. If they took the trouble to watch him before they started spouting off, maybe they wouldn't be so quick to wag their fingers at me over his head.

That chair is like part of his body, and wheeling is as easy for

him as walking is for me. He doesn't get tired on the flat, any more than I do, and when he's going uphill he paces himself. On a roll, he's like a long-distance swimmer, with all the power in his arms and upper body as he glides along.

Watch really closely and you'll see that on the sloping edge of a pavement he'll push the downhill wheel just a little bit harder so that he doesn't veer off to the side. If there's a crack or a low kerb, he'll give a little extra push to get over it, and he'll lean back a bit to shift the weight off the castors at the front of the chair.

You'll see how he can get through narrow spaces, maybe with no more than a few centimetres to spare on each side. He'll never scratch a parked car, or scrape a wall or hit a doorframe. But he won't slow down either, to try and work out if he can get through. He just knows.

When he had his old chair he used to let me have a go on it sometimes, but I was rubbish! He doesn't let me go on his new one. It's blue and silver, and it's made of aircraft-grade aluminium, so it's light and easy to steer.

Last Thursday was one of those days when a well-meaning person spoilt the race. Ricky and I had just finished playing football with some other boys in our class. I was already a bit tired, but as Ricky does the reffing he was as fresh as a daisy. I had the bandstand in sight up ahead and Ricky not far enough behind for comfort. Suddenly this old woman stepped out in front of me, blocking the path. "You should be ashamed of yourself, young man!" she said. "What about your friend?"

My friend looked okay to me, pushing steadily on up towards us, grinning.

I didn't want to be rude, but I didn't want to hang around either, so I ducked past the woman and raced on up towards the bandstand. Too late!

I was only halfway down to the lake when I heard the whirring of wheels behind me, and Ricky went gliding past.

At the bottom of the hill, Ricky took the curve easily and pushed smoothly onto the flat path round the edge of the lake. There was a small rise over the bridge at the far end that would slow him down, but I knew I wouldn't catch him. When I got to the Carlton Street gate he was waiting for me. "Hard cheese, Sam!" he said, grinning. "Shall we go back to yours now and play Road Race, or are you too scared I'll beat you?"

He was joking, of course. Nobody beats me at Road Race!

We went round to the back of the house because we've got a ramp up to the patio doors that my dad built when Ricky first had his accident. It was ages ago, but I can still remember it as if it was yesterday. I can remember when Ricky used to walk on his feet, which is a very strange thought. We were halfway up this cliff on a beach somewhere. Our two families were on a day out together. We'd done the hard bit, and then Ricky goes, "Race you to the top!" Some things never change.

The house was empty, but the computer was on and Abbie's stereo was blaring out upstairs. I went up to tell her to turn it down. She wasn't there. She must've come home and gone out again. Typical Abbie! She's supposed to be in charge until Mum and Dad get in, so it's just as well I don't really need looking after. Some people hate their big sisters, but I think Abbie's okay. I don't mind that she thinks she's cool and she talks down to me quite a lot; I think it's funny. She's in Year 9, but I know she still sleeps with her teddy!

I turned the music off and went back downstairs. Ricky was ready to play Road Race. You would have thought he'd be really good at it. I mean, it's what he does all the time, slowing and steering round corners, speeding up on the straight, getting through gaps, watching out for obstacles, making a little adjustment with one hand or the other. But he just makes stupid mistakes.

He had bounced off the barrier and got bogged down in the mud when we heard a blip, and noticed that Abbie was on Net Messenger. I didn't know her password, so I never normally got to see who she was chatting to on-line. "Let's have a look," I said.

Ricky didn't think we should, but then he hasn't got a big sister. It's always handy having some ammunition. I paused the game and clicked on the icon.

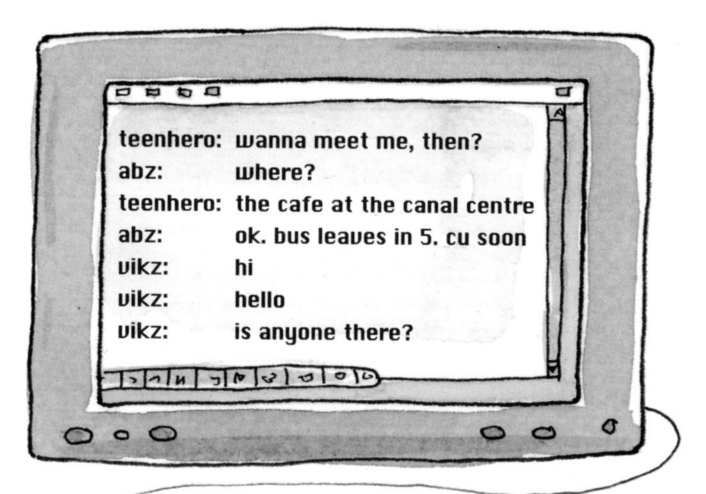


"That's where she is, then," Ricky said. "Who's Teenhero?"

I shrugged. "Let's go to her list of contacts and see if we can work it out."

Abbie's friends weren't very original. They had all just shortened their own names and put a z on the end. There was Emz, Vikz, Sooz, Carlz, and Gemz. And then there was Anto. I frowned. I thought she had got rid of him ages ago. She had met him in a chatroom and they had talked about music for a while. He said he was fifteen, blonde and keen on the same bands as her, but I always thought there was something fishy about him. Now here he was among Abbie's contacts. And then there was Teenhero. Had Abbie picked him up in a chatroom, too? If she had, surely she wouldn't be stupid enough to go and meet him?

Ricky scrolled back through the conversation …

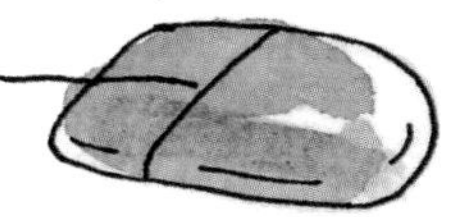

"It can't be one of her friends," Ricky said. "They all know where she lives." I was starting to have a really bad feeling. I got out my mobile and sent Abbie a text. She would probably just tell me to get lost, but I didn't care. A few seconds later, we heard Abbie's mobile bleep in her room upstairs. It must still be in her school bag, or somewhere in the heap of uniform she'd left in the middle of her floor.

For some reason, the sound of Abbie's mobile in her empty bedroom really freaked me out.

"Let's think this through," Ricky said. "Let's stay calm and think it through."

But I didn't feel calm, and when I thought about it, all I could see were newspaper headlines in my head, bad scary headlines that I couldn't blot out.

The clock said 4.35. There wasn't another bus for twenty minutes. It would be quicker to go on

foot, specially if I took the shortcut through Grayson's alley and along the towpath to the bridge.

"What are you thinking?" Ricky asked.

"I'm going down there to make sure she's okay," I said, jumping up. "It'll only take fifteen minutes if I run."

"It's downhill nearly all the way," goes Ricky. "If it takes you fifteen minutes, I bet I can do it in ten."

He didn't wait for me to answer, but started backing away from the computer and turning his chair. "Go on then," he said. "I'll catch up with you."

I ran out the front door and sprinted up to the corner.

Then I turned into Carlton Road and raced along the edge of the park. When I got to the Mini-Mart I glanced back, but there was no sign of Ricky yet. A man came out with a carrier bag full of stuff, and I thought perhaps I should tell him. But tell him what? That my silly sister had gone off without leaving a note to say where she was going? She did it all the time! Probably, there was nothing to worry about. But what if …

I set off again up Union Street and down

Hanger Lane. What if Teenhero turned out to be some weirdo? What if there weren't many people around at the canal centre, and Abbie had no one to turn to for help?

By the time I got to the Cut I was really tired and my heart was pounding. The Cut is a wide straight path that runs between two big houses and brings you out onto Grayson's Alley. There is a concrete post in the middle of the entrance to stop cars going down it. I leaned on the post for a few moments, trying to catch my breath. If Ricky took the corner too fast he could be in trouble. But Ricky would have to look after himself.

I ran through the Cut to the end, and turned into Grayson's Alley, glancing back just in time to see Ricky slide his chair neatly between the wall and the post.

Grayson's alley is much narrower than the cut. The last time I had been down it was in the summer and the edges had been so overgrown you could hardly get through. But the plants had all died back. The garden fences and walls on the left were bare and the tall chain link fence on the right wasn't covered in creepers any more. You could see the woods behind it, sloping gently down towards the canal.

After a couple of hundred metres, the gardens ran out and the path veered sharply to the right, turning almost completely back on itself and dipping down through the woods. I heard Ricky's wheels and jumped clear just in time. He shot past me, going too fast, but I knew the path flattened out later so he would have a chance to slow down before he got to the towpath at the bottom. Seeing Ricky rolling easily away from me made me feel more tired than ever, but I couldn't stop now.

The canal path was straight and flat, only slightly higher than the level of the water. Not so long ago the canal had just been a muddy ditch full of old shopping trolleys, with a few derelict warehouses on a broken wharf. Now the council had cleaned it up and turned the warehouses into a small shopping centre. I could just make it out on the far side of the canal, beyond the bridge.

My feet felt like lumps of lead, but seeing the canal centre spurred me on. Soon I could see the café parlour with its picnic tables on the paved area outside. There were loads of people about, but I couldn't see Abbie among them.

I overtook Ricky just before the bridge. There were some steps up to the bridge, and I knew he would need a hand, but I didn't want to stop.

"You go on," he yelled. "Don't wait!"

I raced up the steps and over the bridge. I burst into the café parlour. Everyone looked round. The place was full of people. But Abbie wasn't there.

Suddenly, I heard a loud whistle. I went back outside and onto the bridge. I saw Ricky on the far side, with his referee's whistle in his mouth. He let it drop out and yelled at me. "I know where they are!" he said. "I saw them go into the gardens!"

I ran back through the arch beside the canal centre into the gardens. Abbie was sitting on a bench with a boy. He was about the same age as her. I had half expected him to be at least fifty, with a beer gut and a seedy smile. I yelled her name, and they both looked round. I thought I recognised him from somewhere.

Abbie was furious. "What are you doing here?" she said.

I was still working out what to say, when Ricky arrived.

"Are you two spying on me?" Abbie demanded.

She saw Ricky and I exchange a glance, and then she sat back and crossed her arms. She didn't have to say a word. We told her everything – about reading her messages, and trying to guess who Teenhero was, and thinking she'd gone to meet some creep off the Internet. She was really angry. "What kind of an idiot do you take me for?" she said. "If you must know, this is my boyfriend, Jason. He's in my class."

"Your boyfriend?" I said. "Why didn't you tell me you had a new boyfriend?"

"Because I knew you'd just be embarrassing like you were last time. Now go home and grow up!"

As we left the gardens I looked back and I saw Abbie and Jason holding hands, not talking to each other, which is exactly what she's like with all her boyfriends. I felt a bit of a fool.

* * * * *

Thinking about it, I could understand why Abbie was cross with me, but I couldn't see why Ricky seemed cross, too. He hardly said a word to me all the way home.

The game was still on the computer. Ricky finished his race. He flew round the course in record time, not making a single mistake. I couldn't believe it – he beat me!

"Are you angry with me?" I asked.

He nodded. "It was downhill nearly all the way to the canal centre, but you got there first," he said. "You've been letting me win when we race through the park. You must've been."

I shook my head. Had I been letting him win? I didn't mean to. "Well, what about Road Race?" I said. "It looks like you've been letting me win at that!" We looked at each other in surprise. Maybe we had been slowing down for each other. And maybe that was okay.